Invitations to Personal Reading, Set B
Curriculum Foundation Classroom Library
Scott, Foresman and Company

Books for Reading Aloud	
Bedtime for Frances	Russell Hoban
Big Cowboy Western	Ann Herbert Scott
The Boats on the River	Marjorie Flack
Come Again, Pelican	Don Freeman
The Cow Who Fell in the Canal	Phyllis Krasilovsky
Make Way for Ducklings	Robert McCloskey
Mommy, Buy Me a China Doll	adapted by Harve Zemach
Mousekin's Golden House	Edna Miller
Mr. Rabbit and the Lovely Present	Charlotte Zolotow
Wake Up, Farm!	Alvin Tresselt

Books to Enrich the Content Fields	
ABC of Buses	Dorothy Shuttlesworth
The Big Book of Real Trains	illustrated by George J. Zaffo
Chicken Little Count-to-ten	Margaret Friskey
Paint All Kinds of Pictures	Arnold Spilka
We Like Bugs	Gladys Conklin

Books for Independent Reading	
The Friendly Animals	Louis Slobodkin
Green Eyes	A. Birnbaum
Have You Seen My Brother?	Elizabeth Guilfoile
I Can Fly	Ruth Krauss
Little Raccoon and the Thing in the Pool	Lilian Moore
My Red Umbrella	Robert Bright
Play With Me	Marie Hall Ets
The Rain Puddle	Adelaide Holl
The Snowy Day	Ezra Jack Keats
What's That Noise?	Lois Kauffman

OTHER BOOKS BY ALVIN TRESSELT
ILLUSTRATED BY ROGER DUVOISIN

SUN UP

AUTUMN HARVEST   WAKE UP, CITY!

FOLLOW THE WIND   FOLLOW THE ROAD

"HI, MISTER ROBIN!"   JOHNNY MAPLE-LEAF

THE FROG IN THE WELL   I SAW THE SEA COME IN

TIMOTHY ROBBINS CLIMBS THE MOUNTAIN

UNDER THE TREES AND THROUGH THE GRASS

WHITE SNOW, BRIGHT SNOW—*Caldecott Medal winner*

WAKE UP, FARM!

by ALVIN TRESSELT

Pictures by ROGER DUVOISIN

LOTHROP, LEE & SHEPARD CO., INC., NEW YORK

Special Scott, Foresman and Company Edition
for the **Invitations to Personal Reading** Program

This edition is printed and distributed by Scott, Foresman and Company by special arrangement
with Lothrop, Lee & Shepard Company, Inc., New York, New York 10016.

To Ellen Victoria and India Rachel

All through the night, while the bright stars shine
in the sky, everything sleeps.
Birds in their nests and cows in the fields.
Horses in barns and children in their beds.
Now it is time for the sun to come up, and the sky grows bright.
First one, then two, then all the birds
begin to sing their morning songs.
Wake up, Farm!

The big fat rooster
hears them and he hops up
on the fence post.
Cock-a-doodle-doo! he crows.
Wake up, Farm!

Cluck, cluck, cluck, the chickens wake up.

They hop down on the ground and start to eat corn.

The horse wakes up in her stall and licks

her baby colt behind the ears.

The white ducks waddle out of the bushes.

They wiggle their tails and jump into the brook for a swim.

Quack, quack, quack!

Wake up, Farm!

Grunt, grunt. The roly-poly pigs wake up and root about their pen looking for breakfast.

The gray goose sticks her long neck out of her nest
in the grass and looks around.

Honk, honk, honk!

Wake up, Farm!

Then high in the apple tree the turkey wakes up, too.

He ruffles his feathers and calls,

Gobble, gobble, gobble!

Wake up, Farm!

The donkey hears all the noise and opens his big brown eyes.

He looks very sleepy as he wiggles his long soft ears.

Now the sheep and baby lambs come out of the sheepfold to eat the wet shiny grass.

The strutting pigeons fly out of the dovecote

and circle over the big red barn.

Coooo, coooo, coooo!

Wake up, Farm!

With a big stretch the tabby cat wakes up.

She purrs as she gives her kittens their morning bath.

Here is the dog, wide awake and barking at a noisy chipmunk.

Bow, wow, wow!

Wake up, Farm!

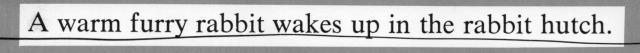

A warm furry rabbit wakes up in the rabbit hutch.

He twitches his wiggly nose as he eats a carrot for breakfast.

Buzz, buzz, buzz!
The buzzy bees come out of their hives
and buzz around the pink clover.

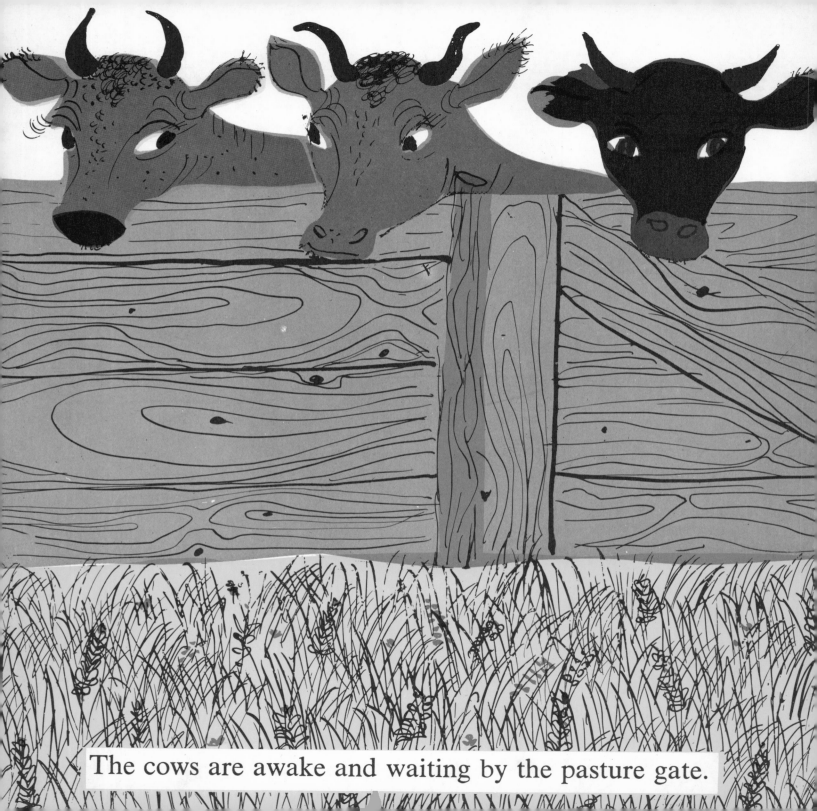

The cows are awake and waiting by the pasture gate.

Moo, moo, moo! It's time for milking!

And here comes the farmer with his shiny milk pails just as the sun comes over the hill.

At last a little boy in the big farmhouse wakes up and stretches.

The birds are singing and the animals are calling.

The bright morning sun is shining in the window.

And mother calls from the kitchen, "Breakfast!"

Another day has begun. Good morning!

DRAGONS AND OTHER CREATURES

Chinese Embroideries of the Ch'ing Dynasty
by
Katherine Westphal

Lancaster—Miller Publishers Berkeley, California 1979

Other titles in the Lancaster - Miller Art Series:

California Murals
text by Yoko Clark and Chizu Hama
Photographs by Marshall Gordon
ISBN 0-89581-106-0

Colored Reading
The Graphic Art of
Frances Butler
ISBN 0-89581-011-3

Mel Ramos: Watercolors
ISBN 0-89581-009-3

Buttons: Art in Miniature
by Stefan O. Schiff
ISBN 0-89581-013-1

The Mad Monk
by Lewis Lancaster
ISBN 0-89581-017-4

The line illustrations throughout this book are the work of
the author, Katherine Westphal.

Copyright © 1979 Lancaster-Miller Inc.
3165 Adeline St.,
Berkeley, California 94703

ISBN 0-89581-012-3

Library of Congress Catalog No. 79-90151

Acknowledgement is made to Mr. and Mrs. Clyde L. Juchau
for assistance in the production of this book.

CONTENTS

PREFACE

This book may be a sentimental journey for me, but it reflects my desire to discuss Chinese embroidery. We owe it to a people constituting one-fourth of mankind, to know more about their arts, especially their love of color and their sense of perfection extending even to the smallest detail.

I owe a debt of gratitude for some knowledge about things Chinese to two primary sources: the men and women who made accessible to me the textile collection of the University of California (Berkeley) and Princess Der Ling's *Two Years in the Forbidden City.*

The textiles are part of a collection I used for design-teaching at the University of California in Davis before my retirement. They have been loved and studied by many generations of selected students and teachers, and have heightened their awareness of textiles and respect for man's skill and imagination with fiber. I am grateful to those whose generosity made these precious pieces available for study, and I thank the donors: Albert Bender, Harriet Foster Brewer, Anson Blake, and others. The collection is housed at the Lowie Museum of Anthropology at Berkeley.

Two Years in the Forbidden City, which I first read in the thirties, is an account of life at the Manchu court at the beginning of this century: what people wore, what they ate, how they traveled, how they felt about events in their lives. It was written with extreme candor by a member of that court, Princess Der Ling (Mrs. T.C. White), who later lived in Berkeley. In 1944, I almost met her but fate intervened. I dedicate this book to the memory of this charming lady who ate ice cream from jade plates.

I would also like to thank the Faculty Research Grant Committee at the University of California, Davis, for its support.

Katherine Westphal
Berkeley, 1979

INTRODUCTION

Recent events in China, recognition as a world power, relaxation of travel restrictions, and a shift in attitude toward the earlier dynastic periods have renewed interest in things Chinese. From the last dynasty, the Ch'ing (Manchus), 1644–1912, large numbers of costumes and domestic wall hangings are available for study. Museums are beginning to exhibit Chinese textile collections more frequently.

Laymen and textile artists want to know more about the textile skills of embroidery and silk tapestry weaving, not with a desire to duplicate—scale, materials, and skill make this unlikely—but to heighten awareness through understanding the visual-design organization and its relationship to process. In addition, to fully understand the message of Chinese textiles, the symbolic intent is as important as design and process.

These Chinese textiles, like all Chinese arts, speak a secret language comprehensible only to those who can read their nonverbal message. Symbols developed over thousands of years create a visual liaison between the individual and his environment. Understanding this cultural heritage leads to understanding the individual work of art. Much is left to intuitive, personal interpretation, because of the Taoist belief that true meaning lies beyond words.

No two works are exactly alike. This diversity is a basic concept of Taoistic art. The changes are as constant and subtle as the waves, ripples, and undulations of water and cloud. However, there is always repetition in stitch, color, and form. This repetitive consistency heightens interest in the subtle changes. The quality of change appeals to twentieth-century man bored with the tyranny of the machine, the endless exact repetition.

The makers of these textiles have been influenced by the imagery and style of paintings on the Manchu period. The motifs or designs have been drawn on silk and then embroidered in silk. Rigid conventions in the use of dark and light, and the illusion of the third dimension are maintained. These follow closely the conventions observed in the brush paintings of the period in the representation of a mountain, a tree, a flower, a man. Reality is used only as a point of departure.

At first glance the embroideries all look alike. One dragon looks like every other dragon. But on close examination, the variations appear, reflecting the individual craftsman's interpretation of a convention. How does he place a particular stitch? Is it tight and perfect, or loose and expressive? Is it fine or coarse? Does one stitch overlap the next? Is it dull or shiny? How do the materials change? Personal preference plays a large part in the interpretation.

All examples of the embroideries are from robes or hangings used in the imperial court of the Manchus. The Manchu period was a time of lavish decorations, wildly exuberant and filled with symbolism in color and image. Almost every inch of a garment could be covered with dragons, animals, flowers, clouds, and Buddhist symbols. The visual organization of such a garment is a bewildering pattern, too lavish to comprehend. When one image is isolated, understood for its design, its technical intricacy, and its meaning, then that image can be related to the next image, and a more complete understanding is possible.

Customs and Costumes

When the Manchus came from the North in 1644 and became the ruling power in China, they brought with them a style of dress and living characteristic of a nomadic people. The loose flowing robes and curl-toed slippers of the preceding dynasty, the more sedentary, intellectual Ming dynasty, were too cumbersome for the Manchus. As was befitting a nomadic people, the Manchu costume was designed for movement.

The decorated robe was long. It had tight sleeves and long cuffs to protect the hands from cold. Trousers were worn to facilitate riding horses. To add warmth, the sleeveless jackets were layered. The costume was completed by a long topcoat and boots.

Men and women wore similar garments, the robe fastening in a curving diagonal to the right side, under the arm and straight down the side. A woman's robe had only side vents. Both men and women wore leggings or trousers under the robe. Over the trousers, and under the robe, the women wore a skirt with plain panels in front and in back, and pleated sides. The bulk of the layers and the elevated shoes gave the wearer a statuesque appearance.

The most spectacular of the garments is the dragon robe (Plate I). There are two basic types. The more formal Ch'ao-fu robe was used for high mortuary portraits and burials. It was considered incomplete without the P'i-ling, a wide triangular collar with the wide section worn over the shoulders to the back. The robe itself is divided into two sections, with a hip-length coat and a pair of aprons overlapping at the sides. The other type of dragon robe, Ch'i-fu, is a full-length coat. It was the official Ch'ing period costume worn at court and throughout the country by Manchu officials.

These dragon robes are almost completely covered by embroidery. Very little ground remains between motifs. Except for the gold foil, everything is silk, silk satin, or silk damask as ground, silk floss as embroidery, and a silk core as the base for the gold-foil wrapped thread. The organization of designs follows the Chinese concept of the universe. There are three divisions: water, earth, and air. The human figure wearing the robe becomes the central axis. The robe is his shell, the universe. The neck edge is the gate of heaven. The human head thrust through the neck hole is beyond all earthly involvements and concerned only with the spiritual. The divisions of the robe into spaces for water, earth, air; the number, size, and placement of dragons and symbols, and the colors, determine the ownership of the robe as well as its place in time.

The water is always at the bottom edge of the robe as either a very narrow or wide band reaching almost to the knees. It has multicolored stripes that break into waves and foam with lucky symbols splashed about. Above the water in front, in back, and on the sides, the cardinal points, is Mount Meru and other rocks designating the earth. More lucky symbols are tossed about here too. Above all this is the splendor of the air alive with dragons, multitudes of lucky symbols, Buddhist precious things, bats of happiness, cranes of longevity, swastikas, coins, flowers, and ribbons all scattered in a complexity of clouds. It is dense with both visual and symbolic meaning.

The dragon's identity is expressed by placement, number of toes, and number of dragons on the robe. The dragon for the emperor and all of his family down to the third rank is the lung dragon with five toes. Below this rank, the members of the imperial family use the mang dragon with four toes.

In the five-toed dragon family, the full-faced dragon is cheng lung, the side-view dragon is hsing lung, the sea dragon hai lung, and the writhing dragon p'an lung. Since the four-toed dragon is referred to as mang, a full-faced dragon would be cheng mang, the side-view dragon hsing mang, etc. Each dragon has a special place on the robe. Cheng lung is front and back center, top. It is always guarding the flaming jewel (see page 00). The hsing lung dragons are on each shoulder and in front and back center, confronting each other over Mount Meru. Sometimes p'an lung, the writhing dragons, are in the skirt section of the robe. The sea dragon, hai

Queen Mother of the West hanging, detail

lung, is occasionally found in and out of the water, wave, and foam area. Dragon robes have nine dragons, a fortuitous number. The ninth dragon is found under the right flap opening in the skirt section of the robe.

In 1694, ceremonial laws of the Ch'ing dynasty were formulated. A dress code was established for all officials of the court from the emperor on down. This code was revised several times and remained in effect until 1911. Since dragon robes in all their splendor were quite similar, the identity problem was solved by a topcoat with a badge, worn by law over the dragon robe. This coat was a plain dark color, three-quarter length for men, full-length for women. It opened down the front and was unadorned except for an identity badge in front and in back. A circle badge was reserved for the emperor and his family. A square was used by officials. The identity-ranking badges worn by the Manchus were based on badges used in the Ming dynasty. There were nine civil and nine military ranks, represented by a bird for the civil ranks and an animal for the military. A bird or animal at rest indicated first-class status. When the bird or animal was in movement, it indicated second-class status. A woman wore a badge identical to that of her husband. A nice symbolism, easily understood.

The front badge is divided vertically into two sections to facilitate the opening of the topcoat. Usually the badges were embroidered directly on the satin ground, however a number of them consist of several sections. The square is one piece with borders representing water, earth, and air. A separate piece with the animal or bird was then appliqued onto the square. This accommodated rapid changes in rank.

After the turn of the century, a young woman—Princess Der Ling, daughter of the Manchu ambassador to France—spent two years as a lady-in-waiting to the Dowager Empress Tz'u-hsi. She wrote a journal-like account of her life at court, *Two Years in the Forbidden City*. The impact of her change in environment and social patterns is clearly expressed. Although she spent her earliest years in China, she had been educated in France. Suddenly she was placed in the restricted pattern of the Manchu court as a companion-attendant to a woman old enough to be her grandmother. She describes the activity with candor. Her viewpoint is sympathetic to her heritage; however, the cultural pattern was different enough for her to have to learn its ways. In these learning sessions, we too can absorb the ritual, the symbolism, and a great deal about the costumes.

Before the availability of the camera in the last half of the nineteenth century, all visual records were from paintings. Since the dragon robe was the official robe of ancestor portraits, we have little other information. The photographic record has changed all that. The impact of photography on the Chinese court is revealed in an incident related in *Two Years in the Forbidden City*. Apparently, the wife of the British consul asked for an audience with the Empress. At this meeting she told the Empress that she should have her portrait painted as was customary for royalty in Europe. Queen Victoria had many portraits painted. The Empress agreed with some hesitancy and later asked Princess Der Ling about the custom. The Empress was confused because in China a portrait was only painted after death. Several days later, the Empress noticed some photographs on Princess Der Ling's table and asked, "What are these? Portraits?" She

Mandarin identity square, egret, sixth rank, civil, detail

Isle of the Blessed hanging

was told that they were photographs done by the brother of Princess Der Ling. Immediately she wanted to be photographed. Brother and camera were summoned, costumes collected, and the group entered the throne room for the photographs. Afterward, the Empress insisted on watching the whole new magical process: developing, printing, washing. In one of the resulting photographs she is wearing the dragon robe and in the other, her favorite gown of the hundred butterflies (see page 20).

Princess Der Ling's book is fascinating: woven in with descriptions of daily activities at court are descriptions of costumes and style preferences. Yellow was the official color for the dragon robes of the Emperor and Empress of the Manchu dynasty. The Ming dynasty had used red. In general, color of clothing reflected the seasons, with yellow reserved for the Emperor. The Dowager Empress did not like her official dragon robe. She felt it made her complexion look yellow. In one instance, just before an audience with the foreign ministers, she changed to her blue satin, hundred butterfly gown and felt better about her appearance.

This is a brief list describing some of the costumes of the Dowager Empress.

A pale-green satin gown embroidered with the character *shou* ("longevity"), precious stones, and pearls. The jade hair ornaments were a bat on one side, and the character *shou* on the other.

A sea-green satin gown embroidered with white storks, and a mauve-colored short jacket also embroidered with white storks.

A peacock-blue satin gown embroidered with the phoenix in the same positions as the dragons on the gown. Each phoenix has a two-inch string of pearls in its mouth. This gown was worn for the first garden party of the year. It, or one of similar description, is in the Royal Ontario Museum in Toronto, Canada.

A blue-satin gown embroidered with butterflies, and a purple sleeveless jacket embroidered with butterflies. The bottom of the gown is decorated with pearl tassels.

A yellow-satin gown embroidered with purple wisteria, and a blue silk scarf embroidered with the character *shou*. Jade butterflies in the hair with a tassle on one side. This was the dress worn for the painted portrait.

These are descriptions of the most lavish costumes used for formal occasions. Other female members of the court, ladies-in-waiting, wives of princes or high officials, and concubines wore a short jacket with a skirt and trousers. As all costumes, these are heavily decorated. The jacket has wide sleeves and turn-back cuffs. The sleeve edges are heavily decorated with a band approximately four to five inches wide and forty inches long. Two-thirds of the band is decorated. The section to the inside when the arm is crossed in front is plain. Thus if a jacket is shown spread out, the sleeve band decoration is in back. Skirts are embroidered on the sections extending below a jacket or a robe.

Toward the end of the Ch'ing dynasty, the ceremonial laws of 1694 began to break down. The roundel, which had been reserved for the Emperor and his immediate family, began to be used widely as pure decoration. It appeared with symbols other than the nine ranks of the identity badge, butterflies, flowers, cranes (see page 57). It could appear as a single decoration or in typical placement on long robes. Flamboyance and decoration were of primary importance.

Domestic Wall Hangings

Domestic hangings are mentioned in Princess Der Ling's account but with little detail. Costume was of more interest to her. Nevertheless, in the same way costume was coordinated to occasion and season, domestic hangings were fitted to occasion with correct symbolic message. They were used on chairs, as cushions and over cushions, on bed structures, on screens, or as coverings for more personal hangings.

Small, densely covered hangings depicting birds or animals in a landscape were popular. The technical style of embroidery was related to southern Chinese embroidery familiar in the West as Spanish shawls. The Isle of Blest, a mythical home of Taoist immortals in the Eastern Sea, is depicted as a landscape with lakes, rivers, and mountains with birds and animals, especially the crane and the deer (see pages 12, 59, 61, 63 and 65).

Another theme for hangings is the Queen Mother of the West, Hsi Wang Mu (see page 67). She wears a crown, guards the peaches of immortality, and is accompanied by girls known as the jade maidens. The Queen Mother often rides ch'i-lin, the mythical Chinese unicorn, which varies in appearance. It can have a horn, a pair of horns, scales or not, lion mane and tail, hooves or paws. It is usually blue and elegant—a fantastic creature (see frontispiece).

The Stitches

The number of stitches is limited. The satin, the stem, the couching, the knot, and the tent are not different from stitches known in the West. It is the skill, scale, design, and color that produce an embroidery with a different look.

Pattern of couching stitch
Left front showing linear pattern
Right back showing pattern of tying stitch

Embroidery was not women's work alone. The heavier, denser embroidery (such as identity squares) was done by men and boys. Much of the theatrical costuming was also done by males.

Robes were embroidered on an uncut length of silk. There are large numbers of these uncut robes in collections today. Many of them were never made into garments but stored away for future use (see pages 39, 41 and 55).

Two types of satin stitches are used: the regular satin stitch completely crossing the shape from side to side, and the long and short satin stitch for larger areas. This latter stitch places each row halfway up and between the previous row like a bricklaying pattern on its side. This produces a smooth, unbroken surface with short floats. For details, such as carp heads, a regular satin stitch is used (see page 69). Color changes occur according to value—dark, medium, light—and define the illusion of three dimensions. In faces of people, the satin stitch moves completely across the form. In old textiles, this part is often worn or snagged, the long silk float destroyed by abrasion.

A couching stitch is composed of two threads. A heavy element is laid on the surface, and held down by an extremely fine element known as the tying thread. In Chinese embroidery, silk wrapped with gold foil is used for the heavy element. The fine tying thread is usually red. If a change in the color impact of the gold is desired, the fine silk can be changed to a green yellow. The two colors of tying thread create impressions of warm and cool gold. A striped water area in the gold-couched identity badge is also done this way. (see page 47).

The silk wrapped with gold foil is usually laid down in pairs. When a more precise and harder look is desired, it is laid down singly. The fine tying stitch is so regular that the stitches form a pattern across the gold resembling machine stitching (see page 14). It is always wise to turn an embroidery over to the reverse side. This reveals much about the laying down of stitches.

Couching also uses a plied silk as the heavier element. This often replaces the stem stitch as outline or it can be a decorative element in itself as in the case of the Go dog from the Isle of the Blessed hanging.

Crane roundels
Left satin stitch on black satin ground
Right tent stitch on black gauze ground

The knot stitch is known by several names, including Pekin stitch or forbidden stitch. It varies from the French knot, employing only one wrap around the needle. It creates a change in texture, a rough surface in contrast to the shiny surface of the satin stitch. Knot stitches are always packed solidly together. They can be worked in a linear fashion, a color line of knots outlining a form (see page 11). Or they can be worked next to another to form a color mass shading from dark to light. Several embroideries do not follow the linear arrangement, but pack an area solidly between the definite line of the couching.

The tent stitch is used on silk gauze, the summer fabric. It is an embroidery based upon a grid. All its curving lines are made up of tiny, straight lines at right angles to each other.

To illustrate the difference in appearance between satin and tent, two similar roundels have been drawn from the embroideries (see page 15). One is the single motif from an uncut robe length. Notice the curving edges of all shapes—the crane, the clouds, the bats. It employs a fine, densely packed satin stitch. A similar roundel is shown with a tent stitch on silk gauze. The crane in the center is surrounded by butterflies and flowers. Careful examination of the edges of all forms reveals no smooth curving lines. All linear edges are sawtooth, relating to the structure beneath the grid of the gauze.

The mythical creatures—the fish, bat, and birds or animals on the identity badges—tend to follow a consistent treatment in design of scales, curls, feathers. The two white satin hangings (see pages 43 and 45) interpreting the textures of the birds and animals are less stylized. Stitching imitates the texture of the animal coat, curly or straight, sleek or fuzzy. The birds are based on such accurate observations of feather and color pattern that the species of crane, duck, or flycatcher is recognizable. The peacock reveals all the delicacy of the feathered fan of display.

The limited variety of stitches does not produce boredom, but heightens interest in contrasts of texture (rough and smooth) and line (straight and curving). The use of one stitch over another adds visual depth. Dense patches of countlessly repeated stitches against unembroidered ground, express substance and solidity, as well as love or perfection. Such embroideries stimulate the game of looking, seeing, and interpreting. We need to notice technical use of embroidery and subtle modifications of the design in order to derive more complete visual and symbolic meaning.

To a member of the Mandarin Court, these textiles had one meaning. To a communist revolutionary, they have another. To a Western collector, still another. History is constantly being reevaluated. The embroideries take on new meaning through individual observation of and response to the visual message. They are a record of human energy, the significance of which changes with time and interpretation.

A simple chart of symbols is given below, which can be used to help play the game of observation and interpretation. Try to read the message of the textile. What are the stitches? What is the relationship of the images? Trying to understand the meaning of the embroidery will result in a keener judgment of a Chinese textile in a museum or an antique shop. It's a game in which nobody wins and nobody loses. It's a game with oneself and one's own perception.

Let us end reading and begin seeing.

CHART OF SYMBOLS

Fu or the bows
(peaceful collaboration
or embroidery as
a fine art.)

coin
(wealth)

ribbon
(charm)

swastica
(happiness)

jade gong
(felicity)

shou
(longevity)

Eight Buddhist Symbols

endless knot
(abundance)

conch shell
(wisdom)

pair of fish
(conjugal felicity)

vase
(perpetual harmony)

lotus
(faithfulness)

umbrella
(charity)

wheel
(infinite changing)

canopy
(spiritual authority)

18

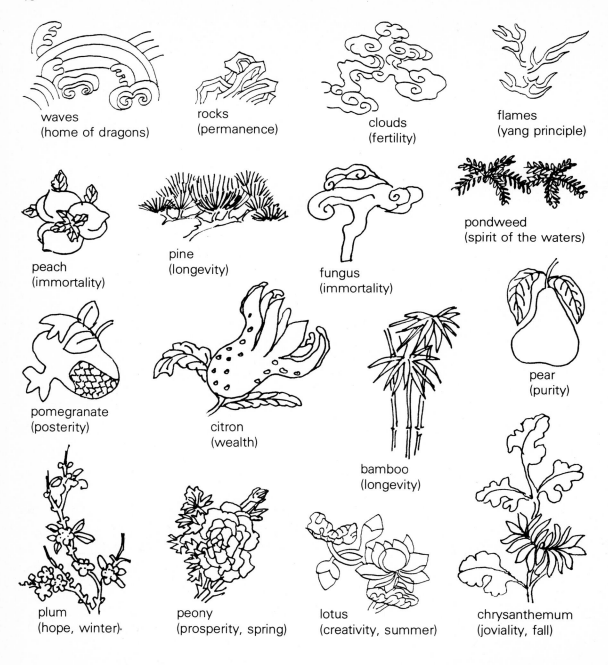

waves
(home of dragons)

rocks
(permanence)

clouds
(fertility)

flames
(yang principle)

peach
(immortality)

pine
(longevity)

fungus
(immortality)

pondweed
(spirit of the waters)

pomegranate
(posterity)

citron
(wealth)

bamboo
(longevity)

pear
(purity)

plum
(hope, winter)

peony
(prosperity, spring)

lotus
(creativity, summer)

chrysanthemum
(joviality, fall)

deer
(longevity)

dragon
(emperor)

lion
(valor)

fish
(abundance)

crane
(longevity)

bat
(happiness)

butterfly
(joy)

phoenix
(empress)

unicorn
(benevolence)

The Dowager Empress T'zu-hsi in her Hundred-Butterfly Robe. Drawn from a photograph in *Two Years in the Forbidden City.*

THE PLATES

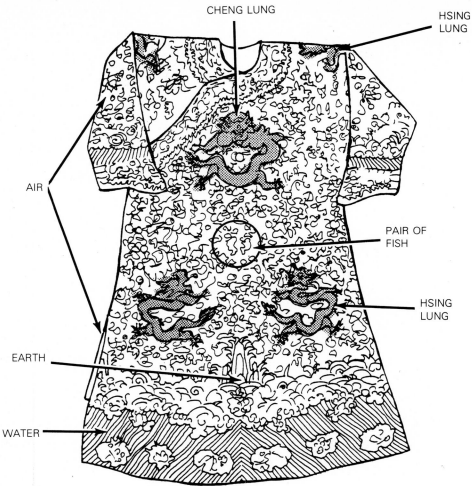

CHENG LUNG

HSING LUNG

HSING LUNG

PAIR OF FISH

AIR

EARTH

WATER

PLATE I
Dragon robe
53'' length, 32 1/2'' sleeve
Blue silk satin ground
Multicolored embroidery, satin, knot and gold couching stitches

A remarkable texture change occurs here in the water band. The flower forms are densely knotted and contrast nicely to the smooth satin stitch of the water. This robe weighs slightly more than four pounds, which attests to the density of the embroidery since silk is a very lightweight fiber.

PLATE II
Dragon robe, detail
53″ length, 32 1/2″ sleeve
Blue satin ground
Multicolored embroidery, satin, knot and gold couching stitches

   This is the cheng lung section. The flaming jewel is embroidered with knots in concentric circles with a light interior and dark exterior.

PLATE III
Dragon robe, detail
53" length, 32 1/2" sleeve
Blue silk satin ground
Multicolored embroidery, satin, knot and gold couching stitches

The precision of the spiral couching stitch to show scales forms a metallic surface, which contrasts with sections of knots and the smooth point shapes surrounding the writhing dragon.

PLATE IV
Dragon robe, detail
53'' length, 32 1/2'' sleeve
Blue satin ground
Multicolored embroidery, satin, knot and gold couching stitches
   This motif is directly below the cheng lung on the robe. It uses a group of Buddhist symbols.
The whole group has a gay, carrousel-like feeling.

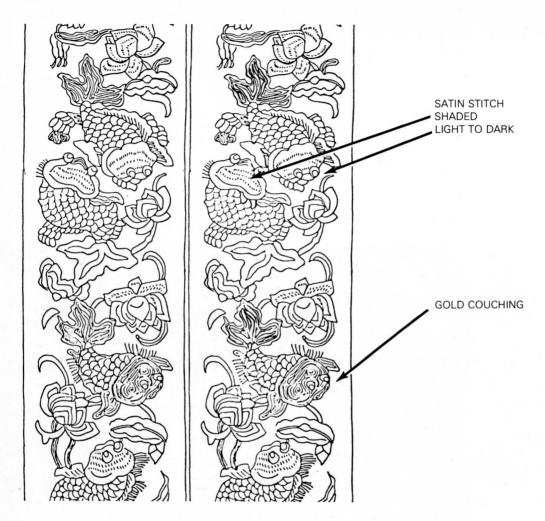

SATIN STITCH
SHADED
LIGHT TO DARK

GOLD COUCHING

PLATE V
Pair of sleeve bands, carp detail
44'' x 4 1/4''
Black silk damask ground
Multicolored satin stitch, some gold couching

It is important to notice the variations in the treatment of the fish. Heads are shaded from dark to light with concentric patterning in gold couching.

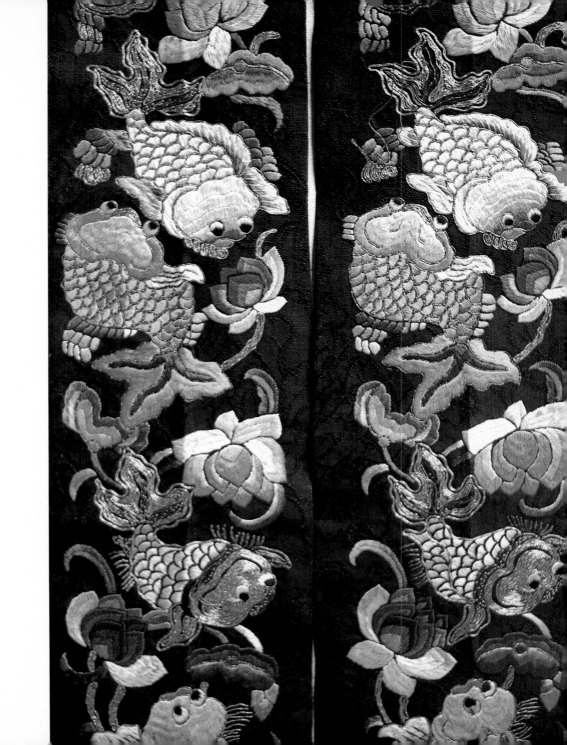

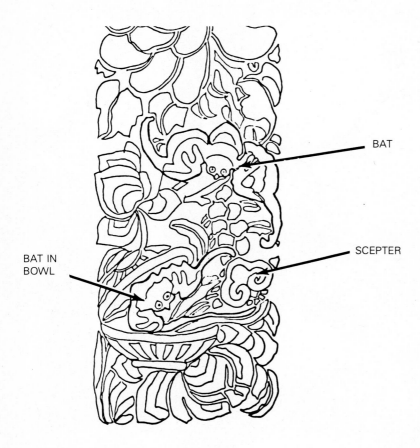

BAT

SCEPTER

BAT IN
BOWL

PLATE VI
One of a pair of bat and flower sleeve bands, detail
39'' x 4 1/2''
Pale-blue satin ground, very faded
Mostly satin stitch in shades of pink, red, blue, gray, and yellow
  Knots are used as an accent shape in the trefoil scepter. Notice the bat in the bowl.

PLATE VII
Dog of Fo hanging
18 1/2'' x 19''
Red satin ground
Gold couching, pale-colored satin stitch

The flowering plants indicate the four seasons. The dog of Fo is playing with a brocaded ball, ribbons swirl from it indicating a lucky charm. This is an excellent example of variations in the use of the couching stitch for hair texture, an outline and a pattern on the ball.

PLATE VIII
Dragon roundel, cheng Lung
10 1/2'' diameter
Black satin ground
Multicolored satin stitch, gold couching
   The border is formed with overlapping clouds in gold couching stitch. The illustration shows the placement of roundels on a long robe. This is from an ancestor portrait.

PLATE IX
Uncut sections for a dragon robe, detail
55'' x 29 1/2''
Red satin ground faded to orange red
Multicolored satin stitch, gold couching

This is an uncut length of silk, which seems to be part of a dragon robe. The body of the cheng mang dragon is white satin stitch with an overlay of blue couching.

PLATE X
Uncut sections for a Dragon robe, detail
55'' x 29 1/2''
Red satin ground faded to orange red
Multicolored satin stitch, gold couching

    The illustration is of the whole length of silk with dragons, water-earth shapes, birds, bats, and cuff shapes. The center of the water-earth sections has unfinished sections showing the black line drawing. This is in the central rock and the tail section of the carp.

PLATE XI
Panel of birds and flowering plants, detail
23 3/4'' x 18 3/4''
White satin ground
Satin stitch with variations of pale colors and lots of white

The illustration indicates the direction of the stitches, the long decorative plumes of the phoenix and the short dense feathers of the flycatcher. Notice the stem stitch in the tendrils of the wisteria.

44

PLATE XII
Panel of birds and flowering plants, detail
23 3/4'' x 18 3/4''
White satin ground
Satin stitch

This detail of the peacock shows great delicacy of the tail feathers spread for display. The entire textile causes delight in recognition of various types of birds and flowering plants. The satin stitch has been modified to show the various feather patterns.

PLATE XIII
Mandarin identity square, Mandarin duck, seventh rank, civil, detail
11 3/4'' x 11 3/4''
Black satin ground
Gold couching

The overlay pattern of the couching on the back of the bird gives a solid metallic texture shape in contrast to the linear design of the bird and sky shape. Note stripes in water.

PLATE XIV
Mandarin identity square, quail, eighth rank, civil, detail
11 3/4" x 12 1/2"
Black silk ground
Knot stitch, gold couching

   The outline of the bird and all symbol forms are gold couching. Forms are filled in with knot stitches following a linear pattern.

PLATE XV
Mandarin identity square, Malay peacock, third rank, civil, detail
8'' x 9''
Black satin ground
Gold and silver couching

The gold on this square is tied in red, the silver in gray. This is an example of a bird embroidered on a separate piece and appliquéd onto another square. Note the difference of embroidery style and skill. This is an example of the two-piece front badge.

PLATE XVI
Mandarin identity square, wild goose, fourth rank, civil
9 3/4'' x 10 1/4''
Black silk ground
Multicolored silk couching
   This is an example of a bird embroidered separately and appliquéd onto the square without identity motive. Bird and square are similar in design and technique.

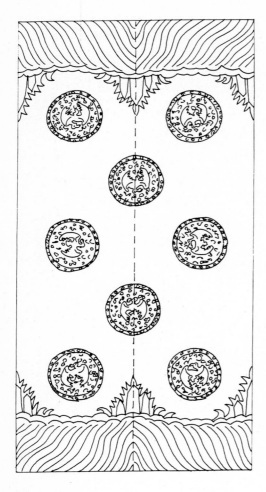

PLATE XVII
Uncut robe with crane roundels
120″ x 61″
Black satin ground
Multicolored satin stitch

This uncut robe shows the placement of the roundels in the air section. Water and earth bands are at each end of the length of silk. Diagram shows placement. Notice the peach of immortality in the beak of the crane. The border of each roundel is composed of bats and the eight Buddhist symbols.

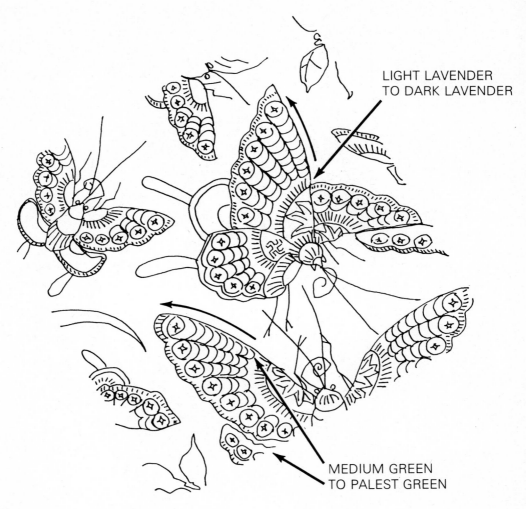

LIGHT LAVENDER
TO DARK LAVENDER

MEDIUM GREEN
TO PALEST GREEN

PLATE XVIII
Butterfly roundel
10 3/4'' diameter
Black satin ground
Multicolored satin stitch

The technical quality of this embroidery is very fine. It has sensitive gradations of color in the wings of the butterflies. The antennae are stem stitched with blue and white plied silk.

PLATE XIX
Isle of the Blessed hanging, elephant, detail
19'' x 14 5/8''
White satin ground
Satin stitch

   The elephant has deep spiral forms at hip and shoulder joints, showing the solidity of the animal.

PLATE XX
Isle of the Blessed hanging, deer, detail
19'' x 14 5/8''
White satin ground
Satin stitch

   A color change gives the deer the spotted pattern. Notice the light spots on medium brown sides changing to black spots on the midsection of the back. This conforms to the natural coloring of the deer. *

PLATE XXI
Isle of the Blessed hanging, dog of Fo, detail
19'' x 14 5/8''
White satin ground
Stem, satin and couching stitches
   The combination of the three stitches creates the look of long hair with curly ends. There is an important scale change in the curls of the tail and the curls of the beard.

PLATE XXII
Isle of the Blessed hanging, ram, detail
19″ x 14 5/8″
White satin ground
Satin stitch and silk couching

   The ram uses a combination of satin stitches as understitching and silk couching in spirals on top to give the texture of fleece. Notice the regularity of the decorative swirls.

PLATE XXIII
Queen Mother of the West hanging
30 1/4'' x 20 1/4''
Red satin ground
Satin stitch in very brilliant color

   The illustration is of the mythical unicorn. It points out the treatment of the scales, a decorative couching stitch over a satin stitch. The piece is finished with decorative bands in blue with a bright green section across the top.

PLATE XXIV
Sleeve with a pair of carp, detail
22 1/2'' x 16
White satin ground
Multicolored satin stitch

This textile has very fine quality in both technique and organization of pattern. It uses the conventional light to dark shading in clouds, bat, foam, waves. Notice the five bats surrounding the eight Buddhist symbols in the illustration.

PLATE XXV
Dragon robe, detail
54'' length, 42 1/2'' sleeve
Dark-blue satin ground
Multicolored embroidery satin stitch and gold couching

Compare the couching stitch on this dragon to the one in Plate II. All embroidery on this robe is tighter and sharper in contrast.

BIBLIOGRAPHY

Cammann, Schuyler. "Notes on the Development of Mandarin Squares," *Bulletin of the Needle and Bobbin Club,* 26:1 (1942).

Carter, Michael. *Crafts of China* (New York: Doubleday, 1977).

Der Ling, Princess. *Two Years in the Forbidden City* (New York: Moffat Yard, 1911; reissue, Dodd Mead, 1924).

Fairservis, Walter A., Jr. *Costumes of the East* (Riverside, Conn: Chatham Press, 1971).

Hawley, W. M. *The Oriental Culture Chart Series,* No. 12, Supplement II: "Chinese Art Symbols" (Hollywood: Hawley Studios, 1949).

Medley, Margaret. *A Handbook of Chinese Art* (New York: Harper & Row, 1964).

Priest, A. and P. Simmons. *Chinese Textiles* (New York: Metropolitan Museum of Art, 1931).

Rawson, P. and L. Legcza. *Tao* (London: Thames and Hudson, 1973).

Scott, A. C. *Chinese Costume in Transition* (Singapore: Donald Moore, 1958).

Vollmer, John. *In the Presence of the Dragon Throne* (Toronto: Royal Ontario Museum, 1977).

This book was set in Universe typefaces
by Mergenthaler Photocomposition at Holmes Typographers,
San Jose; and printed at Grafiche Editoriali Ambrosiane
S.p.A., Milan, Italy.